Girls Got Game

girls' BASKETBALL

Making Your Mark on the Court

by Lori Coleman

Consultant
Dave Preller
Minnesota District Sports Director for Girls' Basketball
Amateur Athletic Union (AAU)

Capstone
press

Mankato, Minnesota

Snap Books are published by Capstone Press,
151 Good Counsel Drive, P.O. Box 669, Mankato, Minnesota 56002.
www.capstonepress.com

Library of Congress Cataloging-in-Publication Data
Coleman, Lori.
    Girls' basketball : making your mark on the court / by Lori Coleman.
    p. cm.—(Snap books. Girls got game)
    Summary: "Describes basketball, the skills needed for it, and ways to
compete"—Provided by publisher.
    Includes bibliographical references and index.
    ISBN-13: 978-0-7368-6821-1 (hardcover)
    ISBN-10: 0-7368-6821-6 (hardcover)
    ISBN-13: 978-0-7368-9926-0 (softcover pbk.)
    ISBN-10: 0-7368-9926-X (softcover pbk.)
    1. Basketball for girls—Juvenile literature. I. Title. II. Series.
GV886.C64 2007
796.323082—dc22   2006021506

Editor: Becky Viaene
Designer: Bobbi J. Wyss
Illustrator: Kyle Grenz
Photo Researcher: Jo Miller

Photo Credits: Capstone Press/Karon Dubke, 10, 13, 18–19, 20–21, 24, 25;
Comstock Klips, back cover; Corbis/Bettmann, 29; Corbis/Gabe Palmer, 17;
Corbis/NewSport/Bart Young, 26; Corbis/NewSport/Greg Fiume, 28; Corbis/
Randy Faris, 15; Corbis/ZUMA/San Antonio Express-New/L. Krantz, cover;
Getty Images Inc./NBAE/Bill Baptist, 22–23; Getty Images Inc./NBAE/Lisa
Blumenfeld, 5; Getty Images Inc./NBAE/Nathaniel S. Butler, 27; Getty
Images Inc./Taxi/Chris Clinton, 8–9; WireImage.com/Kirby Lee, 7

1 2 3 4 5 6 12 11 10 09 08 07

TABLE OF CONTENTS

CHAPTER ONE

SLAM DUNK

Do you thrive on the action of a fast-paced game? Could you spend hours shooting baskets? Joining a basketball team may be the thing for you. But to be a great basketball player you need to be dedicated and willing to practice. And as Lisa Leslie, Sheryl Swoopes, and other basketball greats know, practice pays off.

In 2002, fans cheered as pro Lisa Leslie went up for what people thought would be another lay-up. Slam dunk! Leslie had just made the first dunk ever in a WNBA game. Hoopsters like Leslie have shown girls worldwide how to take their basketball game to the next level. Some day you may be the one slam-dunking your way to success.

Lisa Leslie

So What Is Basketball Anyway?

If you've ever watched or played basketball, you know how quickly the game moves. Basketball games begin with one player from each team in the circle in the middle of the court. To start the game, a referee tosses a ball into the air. Both players quickly jump high. They try to tap the ball to a teammate.

A team's main goal is to score points by sinking baskets. Most youth basketball teams play four quarters. Each quarter is usually eight or ten minutes long. Women's college and professional basketball games are divided into two 20-minute halves.

" Always work on your weaknesses, and continue to work on your strengths. Basketball is a game where you have to continue to work on different aspects of your game. "

—Tamika Catchings, guard for the WNBA's Minnesota Lynx

Taking the Game Outside

Basketball is usually played inside, with five players on each team. But some tournaments move the game from the indoor hardwood floors to the outdoor blacktop courts. Teams may only have one or three players. You can get ready for this 3-on-3 or 1-on-1 action by practicing outdoors with friends.

Keeping Score

Your heart races as you rush toward the basket. You shoot and score! In basketball, most shots are worth two points. Shots taken from outside the three-point line are worth three points. Each free throw is worth one point.

Basketball can be a rough sport, but playing too rough, such as pushing or tripping, will get you a foul. The player on the other team who you foul is awarded up to three free throws. If a player gets more than five fouls, she can't play in the game anymore and is replaced by a teammate. This is called fouling out.

V is for Violation

Violations are different than fouls. If you get a violation, your team will lose possession of the ball.

Examples of violations include:

- traveling: taking steps without dribbling

- double dribbling: dribbling, then stopping, then dribbling again

- missing the basket, rim, and backboard when taking a free throw

- kicking the ball or hitting it with your fist

CHAPTER TWO

HITTING THE COURT

Each of the five players on the basketball team has a specific job to do. Every team has two guards, two forwards, and a center. Which position would you be best at?

Do you like to get right under the basket to nab rebounds and make close shots? If so, you might make a great **center**. The center is usually the tallest, most powerful girl on the team. She stays close to the basket to block the other team from scoring. When centers get the ball, they must quickly shoot or pass to a teammate.

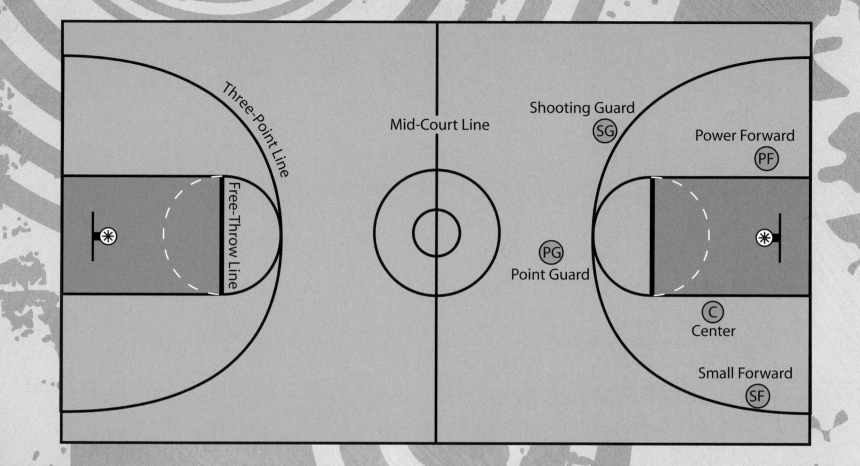

Three-Point Line

Mid-Court Line

Shooting Guard
SG

Power Forward
PF

Free-Throw Line

PG
Point Guard

C
Center

Small Forward
SF

If you're good at lay-ups and rebounding, **small forward** may be the position for you. Small forwards move quickly to steal the ball, shoot, and score points.

While small forwards work hard to score points, **power forwards** try to stop the other team from scoring. From blocking shots to rebounding, power forwards work hard when they're on defense.

Positions Please

Has anyone ever said that you're too short to play basketball? Play guard and you'll prove them wrong. Guards are usually the smallest and quickest players on the team. Most basketball teams have two guard positions: **point guard** and **shooting guard**. The point guard dribbles and moves across the court quickly. The shooting guard must be able to take shots far from the basket. Both guards must pass the ball well and are responsible for setting up plays. They also work hard to stop the other team from scoring.

Teamwork

No matter what position you play, a key part of basketball is teamwork. The best basketball teams are groups of players that know one another's strengths and weaknesses. These players work together and cheer each other on, no matter what.

CHAPTER THREE

GET IN THE GAME

You want to join a basketball team, but where do you start? Joining a community recreational team is a great way to improve your game. You usually don't even have to try out to join the team.

If you're ready for a higher level of competition, join your school's basketball team. This will give you a chance to represent your school and play against girls from other cities.

When your school basketball season ends, you don't have to quit playing. You can join a traveling basketball team. Traveling teams play games against teams from other cities and states during weekends. You'll need to try out to make a traveling team. Work hard and you'll have what it takes!

Camp

Another way to get a lot of practice playing basketball is to attend a basketball camp. Lots of organizations hold mini-camps, day camps, and weekend clinics. Some camps even specialize in certain skills, like shooting. Other camps focus on specific positions, such as point guard or center. From making friends to practicing basketball skills, camps are a fun way to improve your game.

" Work on your ball handling because you'll be playing against some quick guards. Figure out and practice more ways to get your shots off. "
—Katie Smith, forward for the U.S. Women's National Basketball Team

Improving Your Game

After finishing a camp or joining a team, you'll want to practice your moves. Lots of players spend many hours each week practicing.

The more you practice shooting, the more shots you will sink. You can practice lay-ups, jump shots, and free throws. Take shots from different sides of the basket and from different distances. Focus your eyes on the rim or the spot on the backboard you want to hit.

Every shot that doesn't score a basket is a chance for a rebound. Improve your rebounding skills by practicing with a friend. Get into a good position under the basket. Then try to guess where the ball will come off the rim and grab it.

"Offense sells tickets. Defense wins games. But rebounding wins championships.
—Pat Summitt, University of Tennessee Women's Head Basketball Coach and member of the Women's Basketball Hall of Fame"

Dribbling

Dribbling and passing are also important skills to have on the court. When dribbling, look up and not at the ball so you can find open teammates to pass to. Your hands will soon get familiar with the touch needed to dribble well.

Defense

Basketball isn't all about passing, dribbling, and shooting. Defense is just as important. To play good "D," you need to stay low and quick on your feet. Be ready to block, rebound, and steal the ball. Always know where your opponent is. Then try to keep her away from the basket.

Teams use zone and man-to-man defense to stop opposing teams from scoring. For zone defense, you stay in one area of the court and guard any opposing players that come into your area. For man-to-man defense, you guard and follow only one opposing player.

CHAPTER FOUR

BECOMING THE BEST

Years of hard work and practice prepare many women to be part of a high school basketball team. Some of the best high school players are even offered scholarships to play basketball at certain colleges.

But only a small group of the best college basketball players are offered a chance to play professionally. Maybe someday you'll be one of them. But being part of the Women's National Basketball Association (WNBA) isn't easy. It takes dedication and skill, so keep perfecting your moves. Only the best women get a chance to compete at the next level—the Olympics.

Off the Court

The best pro and Olympic basketball players take care of themselves both on and off the court. You need to take care of your body, too. Combine your basketball skills with proper sleeping, stretching, exercising, and eating. Soon you'll be dribbling circles around your opponents.

Getting the right amount of sleep lowers your risk of injuries. Try to get 8 to 9 hours of sleep each night.

Once you're well-rested, you'll be ready to pass, shoot, and score. But, don't forget to stretch first. Loosen your muscles by spending 10 to 15 minutes stretching before each game or practice.

Exercising is a good way to increase your endurance. Jumping jacks and jumping rope will strengthen your legs for lay-ups and rebounds. Running, swimming, and biking will get your body ready to sprint across the court.

Want to be well-prepared for practice or your next big game? Begin your day with breakfast. Some good breakfast options include cereal, toast, fruit, and yogurt. Breakfast will help give you the energy your body needs. Later, have a mid-morning snack to keep your energy level high.

CHAPTER FIVE

PRO PLAYERS

Some of the biggest stars in women's basketball have worked hard to take their game to the next level. These outstanding women have helped make women's basketball the exciting sport it is today.

Forward Sheryl Swoopes helped the Houston Comets win the WNBA Championship from 1997 to 2000. She also won the league's Most Valuable Player Award in 2000 and 2002. Swoopes helped the U.S. Women's Basketball Team win gold medals in the Olympics in 1996, 2000, and 2004.

Sheryl Swoopes

Katie Smith

Katie Smith started playing basketball on a boys' team when she was in fifth grade. Years later, this Minnesota Lynx guard was the first WNBA player to score 500 three-point shots. Soon after setting this record, Smith was traded to the Detroit Shocks team. Smith was on the gold-medal winning U.S. Women's Basketball Team for the 2000 and 2004 Olympics. She believes that always giving her best effort is important. To her fans, Smith says, "Every night I'm going to come out and play hard for you. I just love what I do."

Lisa Leslie

In 2001, Los Angeles Sparks center Lisa Leslie was the first player to be named Most Valuable Player for several WNBA events. She was awarded Most Valuable Player of the WNBA season, WNBA Championship, and WNBA All-Star Game. In 2006, she was still the WNBA's leading scorer (4,732 points) and rebounder (2,540 rebounds). Leslie's outstanding skills have brought lots of extra attention to the WNBA. She says, "I like that I can help to change people's perspectives about what women can and can't do. And when my playing days are over, I hope people will remember me as the most versatile center to ever play the game, man or woman."

Ann Meyers has been the leader for many basketball firsts for women. In 1976, she was a player on the first Olympic U.S. Women's Basketball Team. In 1979, Meyers was the first and only woman allowed to try out for a National Basketball Association (NBA) team, the Indiana Pacers. Although this outstanding player never made the team, it was an honor just to be allowed to try out.

Ann Meyers

Someday you may be the one setting records in women's basketball. Get ready to dribble, pass, and slam-dunk your way to success. Soon you'll be part of a winning team!

GLOSSARY

defense (di-FENSS)—the team that tries to stop baskets from being scored; the defense is the team that doesn't have the ball.

dunk (DUHNK)—when a player jumps above the basketball rim with the basketball and throws it into the net

foul (FOUL)—an action in basketball that is against the rules; pushing and tripping are fouls.

free throw (FREE THROH)—an unguarded shot taken from behind the free-throw line by a player whose opponent committed a foul

lay-up (LAY-uhp)—using one hand to push the ball up and bounce it off the backboard and into the basket

opponent (uh-POH-nuhnt)—a person who competes against another person

FAST FACTS

The first ball used for basketball was actually a soccer ball. The first basketballs were brown. Their color was later changed to orange, so they would be easier for players to see.

Men's basketball became a part of the Olympics in 1936. Women finally got their chance to play in 1976, when women's basketball was added to the Olympics.

The Amateur Athletic Union (AAU) Girls' Basketball now has about 12,000 teams across the country. Each year, about 4,500 of those teams compete to play in AAU National Championships.

READ MORE

Eule, Brian. *Basketball For Fun!* Sports for Fun! Minneapolis: Compass Point Books, 2003.

Hughes, Morgan. *Basketball.* Junior Sports. Vero Beach, Fla.: Rourke, 2005.

Kelley, Brent. *Lisa Leslie.* Women Who Win. Philadelphia: Chelsea House, 2001.

Thomas, Keltie. *How Basketball Works.* How Sports Work. Toronto: Maple Tree Press, 2005.

Wallner, Rosemary. *Sheryl Swoopes.* Sports Heroes. Mankato, Minn.: Capstone Press, 2001.

INTERNET SITES

FactHound offers a safe, fun way to find Internet sites related to this book. All of the sites on FactHound have been researched by our staff.

Here's how:

1. Visit *www.facthound.com*

2. Choose your grade level.

3. Type in this book ID **0736868216** for age-appropriate sites. You may also browse subjects by clicking on letters, or by clicking on pictures and words.

4. Click on the **Fetch It** button.

Facthound will fetch the best sites for you!

ABOUT THE AUTHOR

Lori Coleman has been actively involved in the lives of young people. Lori likes to help kids out in school and in other sports like basketball, cycling, running, and horseback riding. She has written several children's books on the topics of sports and animals. Some of her titles for children include *Play by Play Soccer*, *The American Saddlebred Horse,* and *My Pet Fish*.

INDEX